WASH Those HANDS!

John Townsend

Carolyn Scrace

Soap and bubbles wash off troubles!

Published in Great Britain in MMXXI by
Scribblers, an imprint of
The Salariya Book Company Ltd
25 Marlborough Place, Brighton BN1 1UB
www.salariya.com

ISBN: 978-1-913337-95-7

SALARIYA
SCRIBO · BOOK HOUSE · SCRIBBLERS

1 3 5 7 9 8 6 4 2

A CIP catalogue record for this book is available
from the British Library.

Editor: Nick Pierce

Visit
www.salariya.com
for our online catalogue and
free fun stuff.

PAPER FROM
SUSTAINABLE
FORESTS

Meet the Scribble Monsters!

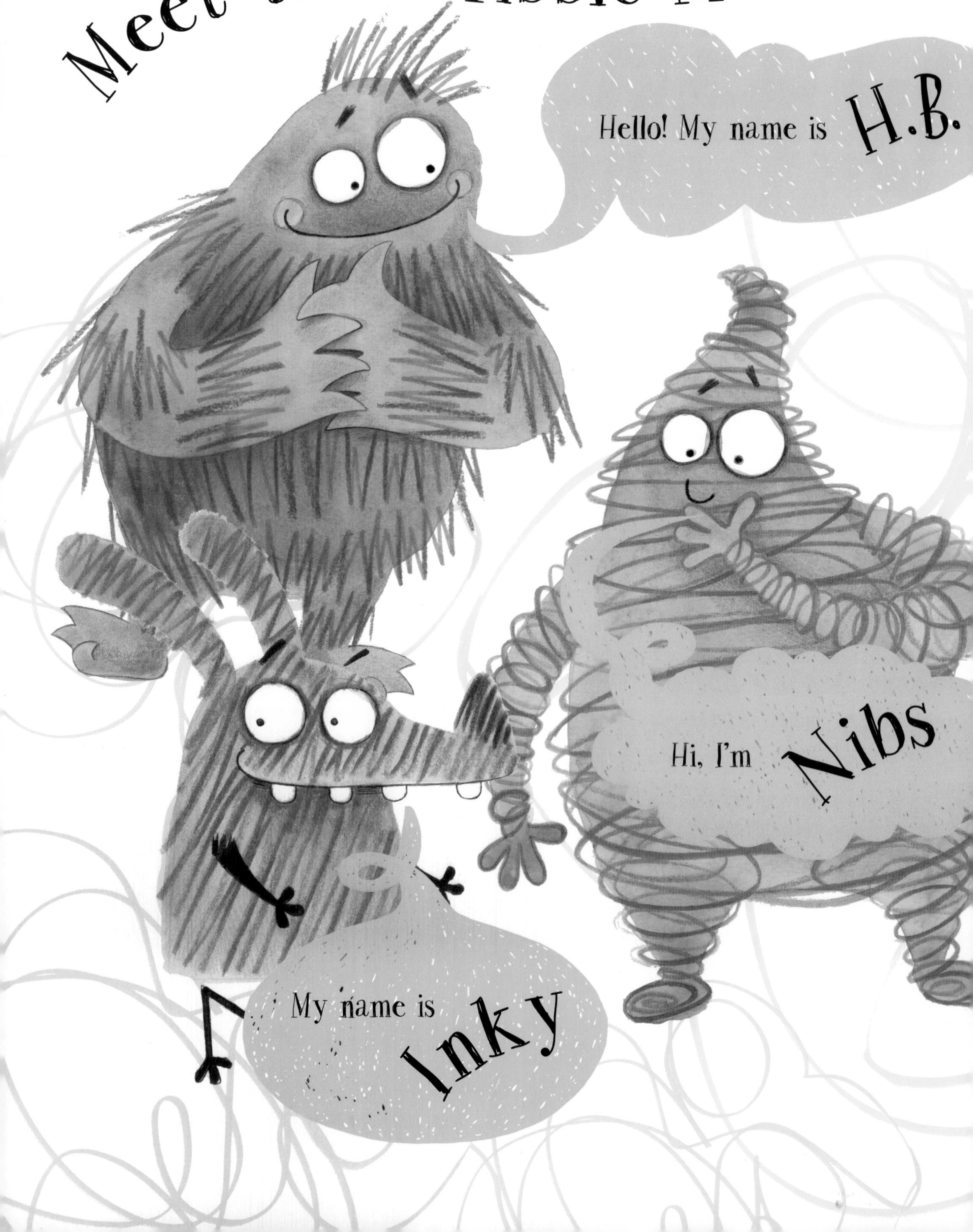

We're the friendly Scribble Monsters,
We scribble lots of lines
And write how manners can be fun
On all our scribbly signs.

Goodbye germs - wash your hands.

I'm being good and washing my hands.

Good manners and safety are in your hands.

Some little children can forget
To leave clean rooms behind them...
We're here to scribble our advice
And find ways to remind them.

Be clean

Think of others

Good manners
show you care

Clean hands
are cool!

Monsters
with
manners

Some children leave their finger marks
Wherever they have been...
So Scribble Monsters like to say,
'Please keep your fingers clean.'

If you're grubby, just get scrubby,
Have a splash and splosh.
It's good to think, 'I'll use the sink
And give those hands a wash.'

N ibs says that the word 'hygienic'
Means 'both safe and clean'.
Wash off all those pesky microbes
That are so small they can't be seen.

AAA CHOO!

These tiny germs can make us poorly
By spreading some diseases.
They sometimes whizz right through the air
As soon as someone sneezes.

Inky asks that when you're sneezing,

Please do use a tissue!
Then throw it in the bin and wash well...
Before I'll want to kiss you!

It shows respect to wash your hands
After you've been sneezing,
By proving that you care for others...
Such manners are so pleasing!

'Germs are clingers – scrub those fingers!'
That's what Pablo thinks.
'Keep them blotless, clean and spotless,
When handling food and drinks.'

No germ lingers on clean fingers,
That's what Blot insists...
'Come to terms with killing germs,
So scrub those hands and wrists.'

As soon as H.B. comes indoors,
He reaches for the taps
And even cleans his fingernails
Where germs can hide, perhaps.

Smudge just loves to have a bath
To soak away all troubles...
Soon dirt and germs will disappear
From paws, among the bubbles.

It's bedtime but before we sleep,
We don't want to forget
To clean those teeth and wash those hands
And get them nice and wet...

Oh, that feels so clean and tingly,
When you're tucked in bed.
Close those eyes, you're snug and spotless...
There's no more to be said!

Goodnight!

All hands to
the pump!

Children who can keep their hands clean
And squirt a squidge of soap,
Get the Scribble Monsters dancing,
'Yay – clean hands give us hope.'

Safe high five!

H.B., Inky, Nibs and Pablo
Know germs won't survive.
When they see you wash your fingers,
They'll mime a safe high five!

Safe high five!

HAVE YOU HEARD THE MAGIC WORDS?

GOOD MANNERS ARE FREE!

Washing hands will never tire us
In our quest to beat the virus!
Be aware – so wash with care!
Don't be mean – keep hands clean!
Don't be smug – scrub the bug!
If you touch – scrub them much!

Children with clean fingers sparkle!

CAN YOU HELP US FIND THE ANSWERS TO THIS QUIZ?

QUESTION 1

What should we always try to do after going to the toilet?

QUESTION 2

What song should we sing twice when washing our hands?

QUESTION 3

AAA CHOO!

What did Inky ask us to do with a tissue after we've sneezed into it?

QUESTION 4

Should we wash our hands after sneezing?

Look at the last page of the book to see if you are right!

MORE MONSTER QUESTIONS

QUESTION 5

What does the word 'hygienic' mean?

QUESTION 6

Should I keep my hands clean when I'm handling food?

QUESTION 7

What do I do as soon as I come indoors?

QUESTION 8

Before we go to bed, what must we remember to do?

Look at the last page of the book to see if you are right!

GOODBYE!

Answers to the quiz:
1   Wash our hands, then rub them dry.
2   'Happy Birthday.'
3   Throw it in the trash.
4   Yes!
5   Safe and clean.
6   Yes!
7   I reach for the taps.
8   Clean our teeth and wash our hands.